Our Money

by Ann Marie Smith

HOUGHTON MIFFLIN   BOSTON

This is a penny.
You can see
Abraham Lincoln.

This is a nickel.
You can see
Thomas Jefferson.

This is a dime.
You can see
Franklin D. Roosevelt.

This is a quarter.
You can see
George Washington.

This is a one dollar bill.
You can see both sides.
Find George Washington.

This is a five dollar bill.
You can see both sides.
Find Abraham Lincoln.

You can see
many important
people on our money.